KU-528-697

✦ A FABER PICTURE BOOK ✦

Mr. Mistoffelees

Written by T. S. Eliot

Illustrated by Arthur Robins

ff

FABER & FABER

Please listen to me and don't scoff. All his Inventions are off his own bat.

There's **no such Cat** in the metropolis;
He holds **all** the patent monopolies

For performing **surprising** illusions . . .

And creating **eccentric** confusions.

At prestidigitation
And at legerdemain
He'll defy examination
And deceive you again.

The greatest magicians
have something to learn

From Mr. Mistoffelees' Conjuring Turn.

Presto!

Away we go!
And we all say: OH!

Well I never!
Was there ever
A cat so clever

As Magical
Mr. Mistoffelees!

He is quiet and small, he is black

from his ears to the tip of his tail;

He can creep through the tiniest crack,

He can walk on the narrowest rail.

He can pick **any** card
from a pack,

He is **equally**
cunning with dice;

He is **always**
deceiving you
into believing
That he's only
hunting for **mice.**

He can play any trick with a cork

Or a spoon and a bit of fish-paste;

If you look for a knife or a fork
And you think it is merely misplaced—

You have seen it one moment,
and then it is **gawn!**
But you'll find it next week
lying out on the lawn.

And we all say: OH!

Well I never!
Was there ever
A Cat so clever

As Magical Mr. Mistoffelees!

His manner is vague and aloof,
You would think there was nobody shyer—

But his voice has been heard on the roof

When he was curled up by the fire.

And he's sometimes been **heard** by the fire

When he was about on the roof—

(At least
we all **heard**
somebody
who purred)

Which is incontestable proof
of his singular **magical powers:**

And I have known the family to call
Him in from the garden for hours,
   While he was asleep in the hall.

And we all said: OH!
Well I never!
Did you ever
Know a Cat so clever . . .

As Magical Mr. Mistoffelees!